MARTHA SPEAKS™

Puppy Dog Tales Collection

D0381949

Based on the characters created by **SUSAN MEDDAUGH**

HOUGHTON MIFFLIN HARCOURT
Boston New York

Contents

For information about permission to reproduce selections from this book, write to Permissions, Houghton Mifflin Harcourt Publishing Company, 215 Park Avenue South, New York, New York 10003.

ISBN: 978-0-544-34117-3 pa

www.hmhco.com

www.marthathetalkingdog.com

Manufactured in China
SCP 10 9 8 7 6 5 4 3 2 1
4500498667

A Pup's Tale

Adaptation by Jamie White
Based on a TV series teleplay written by Allan Neuwirth
Based on the characters created by Susan Meddaugh

MARTHA SAYS HELLO

Hi there!

Be warned, Martha fans: What you are about to read might shock you!

You already know that Martha is a dog who can speak. And speak and speak . . .

7

And you probably know that she's been able to speak ever since Helen fed her alphabet soup. No one's sure how or why, but the letters in the soup traveled up to Martha's brain instead of down to her stomach.

Now, as long as she eats her daily bowl of alphabet soup, she can talk. To her family: Helen, baby Jake, Mom, Dad, and their dog Skits, who only speaks Dog. To Helen's friend Truman. To anyone who'll listen.

Sometimes Martha's family wishes she didn't talk *quite* so much.

But who would want to discourage a talking dog from, well, talking? Besides, her speaking comes in handy. One night, she called 911 to stop a burglar.

So, do you think you know all about Martha? Well, think again. This is the surprising story about Martha's early life in crime.

WHO KNEW?

Martha's good friend Truman didn't know this shocking tale. And he knows *everything!*

It happened like this. Martha and Truman were watching TV at his house. On screen, police chased the bad guys.

"Those crooks aren't very smart," said Truman. "It won't take long for the cops to catch them."

"They always do," said Martha. "Just like they caught me back when I was robbing stores."

Truman's jaw dropped. "Robbing *what?*"

"Stores," said Martha. "Before Helen adopted me, I robbed stores. Well, one store . . . and a museum."

She stood up and yawned.

"I'm off to the park," she said, heading to the front door. "Those ducks don't bark at themselves."

"A store? A *museum*? Robbery? When were
you going to tell me this?"

"It never came up," said Martha. "Maybe
one day I'll write my life story. Then I'll
tell everyone."

"You're going to write your autobiography?"
asked Truman.

"No, my life story," said Martha.

"That's what an autobiography is—a book
someone writes about her own life. Can I help
you write it? Starting with your life in crime?"

"I guess," said Martha. "If you don't mind barking at a few ducks first."

So that's just what they did. They went to the park and barked at ducks.

And then Truman helped Martha write this book. Martha talked. Truman wrote.

Now go on . . . read her surprising autobiography.

MY LIFE IN CRIME
BY MARTHA

I was only eight weeks old, and already behind bars . . . at the animal shelter.

Every day, I sat in my small cage waiting to be adopted. I'd watch humans walk in and out of the animal shelter. But no one wanted to take me home.

Kazuo was in charge of the shelter, just like he is now. He tried to find us dogs good homes. Sometimes he'd point me out to visitors. The first one I remember well was a lady in a fur coat.

How could I forget her? She tried to stuff me into her purse. *Ouch!* I was too big.

"I need a dog that fits!" yelled the lady.

And thankfully she moved on—to the next cage.

The next day, a grumpy man visited.

"I'd like a dog that can do tricks," he said.

I danced in circles for him.

"Is that all it can do?" asked the man.

He moved on, too.

Later, a magician came in. He squeezed me into his top hat. Then he tried to pull me out by my ears. I yelped. *Ouch* again!

"Will her ears grow?" asked the magician.

"Dude," said Kazuo, taking me back from the magician.

"I think you need a *rabbit*."

No one thought I was just right.

All day long, I'd watch pets leave with new owners.

"Give me a chance!" I wanted to shout. "I'll be the best pet on four legs!"

But I couldn't speak. I hadn't eaten alphabet soup yet.

"Don't give up hope, Martha," Kazuo said. "There are still lots of possibilities."

I cocked my head to the side. *Huh?*

"Possibilities are things that can happen," said Kazuo.

At that point, the only possibility I saw was a lifetime behind bars.

"Lots of people want dogs," said Kazuo. "It's possible you might be a police dog."

A K-9 cop! I could just imagine it. I'd direct traffic with my tail and my whistle. There would never be a traffic jam!

"That's just *one* possibility," Kazuo said. "It's also possible you could be a water rescue dog."

Hot dog! I thought. I'd put a stop to any dangerous water tricks. Besides, everyone looks up to a lifeguard.

"Or it's possible you could live with the owner of a bowling alley. You could put your keen sense of smell to use."

Yes! I'd work at the shoe rental desk. When people returned their bowling shoes, I'd sniff out their sneakers for them.

These possibilities all sounded great. But none of them was what I really, *really* wanted. What I yearned for was a home and family of my own.

Then one morning, things began to look promising.

THE LITTLE RED-HAIRED GIRL

It all started when a family visited the animal shelter, looking for a pet.

"A cat?" Kazuo said. "We have plenty. Follow me."

The grownups walked past my cage. But the little girl stopped. She had the nicest smile.

"Hi!" she said.

The moment I saw her, my tail wagged with joy. Can you guess who she was?

23

"Helen!" her mom called from across the room.

Yes, she was my very own Helen!

Mom pointed at an orange cat. "Look. Isn't he cute?"

"I guess," said Helen. "But look at this puppy!"

Could she be my new owner? I gave her cheek a slobbery kiss.

"That's Martha," said Kazuo.

"Martha!" said Helen. "I like her. Let's adopt her!"

"But, honey," said Dad, "that's not a cat."

"She's better than a cat," said Helen.

I knew then that this was a girl after my own heart.

"Helen," said Mom, walking over. "We've discussed this. Don't you recall? Dogs need a lot of care."

"Yes, but . . ."

Mom placed a hand on Helen's shoulder. "I'm sorry. Martha looks sweet, but a puppy is too much work right now."

Now things *didn't* look promising. And they were about to get worse. A *lot* worse.

A SHOEBOX-SIZE DOG

It's not fair, I thought after Helen left. *I should be home with that little red-haired girl. Instead I'm stuck in this cage.*

The shelter was quiet. The animals snoozed. Behind his counter, Kazuo read a magazine. The peace didn't last long.

A lady wearing a purple dress and lots of jewelry burst through the door. She was with a man in a suit. The man was quiet. The lady was not.

She wore plastic bangles that rattled when she moved her arms. She spoke in a loud voice. And although Kazuo was right in front of her nose, she banged the desk bell.

DING!

Kazuo jumped.

Ding! Ding!

"Excuse me—do you work here?" the lady demanded.

Kazuo looked around. "Uh . . . yes?"

"Carlotta Bumblecrumb!" the woman said, introducing herself.

"What can I do for you, Ms. Crumble-bum?" asked Kazuo.

"It's *Bumblecrumb!*" she snapped. "I'm here to adopt a dog. It should be the size of a shoebox."

"Hmm," said Kazuo. "Follow me."

Kazuo tried to show her a poodle. But she peeked into my cage.

"You look promising," she said to me. "And when I say you look promising, I mean I think you'll work out just right."

She read my nametag. "Can 'Martha' be trained?"

"Trained to do what?" asked Kazuo.

"None of your—" began the lady. She slapped her hand over her mouth. "*Oops!* I mean . . . I recall that as a child I owned a dog that did tricks. Ever since then, I've yearned for another."

Kazuo raised an eyebrow. "Why does Martha need to be the size of a shoebox?"

"So I can push the mutt through a hole about—*oops!*" said Carlotta Bumblecrumb. Again she stopped midsentence. "I mean . . . because I've already built a tiny doghouse. Yes, I built it out of a *shoebox*. I need a pooch that will fit inside."

"You know she's going to grow, right?"
said Kazuo.

"Then I'll build a bigger doghouse," she
said. "How much do you want for her?"

"We don't charge you to adopt a pet."

"Perfect," she said.

She opened my cage. *Rattle, rattle* went her
bangles. Her hands reached for me.

At that moment, I yearned to speak
Human. "Consider the cat!" I'd say. "Cats fit
perfectly into shoeboxes! Think it over, lady!"

I backed away, and Kazuo noticed.

"Uh, I just recalled something," he said
quickly. "Martha hasn't had all her shots yet.
You'll have to come back in a few weeks."

Carlotta Bumblecrumb scowled.

"I see," she said, forcing a smile. She waved
goodbye to me. "Ta ta then, sweet cheeks!
Mama will be back soon!"

With that, luckily, the loud scary lady and
her silent companion left. Kazuo and I let out
a sigh. Phew.

But I was still sad and alone. And I wasn't the only one. At home, Helen was heartbroken, too.

I know what you're thinking. How can I narrate Helen's side of the story if I wasn't there? Well, Helen told it to me. So now I can narrate it for you . . .

DOGGY NIGHTMARE

"Please, please, please!" Helen begged. She hopped in front of the sofa, where her mother was trying to read. "I promise I'll take care of the puppy!"

Mom put down her book.

"That's what you said about Goldie," she said. "Do you recall what happened to her?"

When Helen was five, she had a goldfish named Goldie. All day long, Goldie did nothing but swim in circles. Around and around the fishbowl she went.

Goldie looks bored, Helen thought. *She needs a vacation.*

So the next time Helen's family went to the lake, Helen secretly brought Goldie along, too. *Plop!* She dropped Goldie into the water for a quick swim. After a few minutes, Helen said, "Come back now, fishy." But Helen never saw Goldie again.

(This scene from Helen's past is what Truman calls a flashback. But if he doesn't stop interrupting me to explain what a word means, I'll never finish my story!)

"I didn't know Goldie wouldn't come back," Helen told Mom. "I'll be more careful with a dog. *Please?*"

"Helen, we went over this at the shelter today," said Mom. "A dog is a big responsibility. You need to wash it, walk it . . ."

"I'll wash her. I'll walk her," said Helen, hopping higher. "*Pleeeeease?*"

"No," said Mom. "I'm sorry."

Helen stopped hopping. As the days passed, she stopped begging, too. She didn't stop missing me, though. One look at the refrigerator door would tell you that. It was covered with her drawings of me.

One day, Helen began to write my name
on her latest picture. Mom and Dad watched
from the doorway.

"How do you spell 'Martha'?" asked Helen.
Mom looked at Dad. "I give up," she said.
Dad nodded.

Helen's face lit up. "Do you mean—?"

"Yes," said Mom, smiling. "You can have Martha."

"THANK YOU!" shouted Helen.

She hugged Mom's legs. She threw her arms into the air. She ran in circles through the house.

"YAY! WHOO-HOO! YIPPEEEEEEEE!"

Mom and Dad covered their ears.

"We'd better go first thing in the morning," Dad said.

The next morning at the shelter, I lay in my cage, watching a collie eat kibble. *Ho-hum. Bor-ing.*

But then . . . Kazuo ran in wearing a smile.

"GUESS WHAT, MARTHA?" he shouted. "YOU'RE BEING ADOPTED!"

Holy macaroni! Those were the sweetest words I'd ever heard. I leaped to my paws. *That little red-haired girl had come back for me!*

Or so I thought.

Kazuo pointed to the doorway. "Martha, say hello to your new owner, Miss Eudora Biddlecomb!"

My tail stopped wagging.

Eudora Biddlecomb was no little red-haired girl.

"Hello, sweet little poochie," she said in a shaky old lady's voice. She tickled me under the chin. "We're going to be pals, you and I. Hee hee hee. I knew I liked you before."

Kazuo raised his eyebrows. "Before?"

The old lady's hand covered her mouth.

"*Oops!* I mean . . . before I came in. I had a feeling I'd like what I saw here," she said, winking at me. "And I was right. I'm going to love owning you."

Before I could even woof goodbye to Kazuo, the old lady whisked me out the door. Suddenly she didn't need to lean on her cane anymore. Like an Olympic runner, she hustled us into a pink limo parked outside.

"Good poochie," she said, slamming the car door.

Just before it shut, I saw an awful sight. Helen and her parents were walking into the shelter! I had missed them by seconds.

"ARF!" I barked. "ARF! ARF!"

"QUIET!" shouted the old lady.

Her voice was different. It was familiar. It was LOUD.

Eudora Biddlecomb took off her gray wig.

"Ha! Surprised to see me again?" said Carlotta Bumblecrumb. "You're mine now. Tomorrow you start working for me."

This was a doggy nightmare. Even worse than the one I had about being chased by a giant head of lettuce.

"Home, Mr. Stubble!" she ordered the driver.

I scratched at the back window and watched Helen disappear. Of all the promising possibilities I had imagined, this was not how I thought I'd end up.

HOME HORRIBLE HOME

At the shelter, Helen stood next to my empty cage. (I'm narrating Helen's story again. Can you tell?)

"She's . . . gone?" asked Helen, her voice trembling.

"I'm sorry," said Kazuo. "I wish you'd arrived sooner."

"Martha," Helen said softly.

She felt like she was about to cry. And then she did.

Meanwhile, where was *I*?

I was lying on the cold floor of Carlotta Bumblecrumb and Mr. Stubble's warehouse. My new home wasn't exactly what I'd hoped for. There was no comfy couch. No chewies. No chops. And no Helen.

Instead I saw a broken table, hard chairs, an old TV, and boarded-up windows.

"Time to begin your training, pooch!" said Carlotta Bumblecrumb. She took a red ball from her purse. "See this? When I throw it, you're going to fetch it. Got that?"

She threw the ball. "Fetch!"

I watched it bounce away. *Why does she want me to fetch that little red ball?* I wondered.

"Go on!" she ordered. "It's a game. FETCH THE BALL!"

Let's play another game, I wanted to say. *How about "Fetch the MEATball"?*

"Mr. Stubble, show this mutt how it's done!" said Carlotta Bumblecrumb.

She tossed another ball.

"Watch this, pooch," she said.

"First, he'll run. Second, he'll get the ball. Finally, he'll bring it back to me! A proper sequence, see?"

Mr. Stubble ran on all fours with his tongue hanging out. He fetched the ball with his mouth. He looked like a very silly dog.

"Good boy, Mr. Stubble!" she said.

She popped a cookie into his mouth.

Hey! Nobody said anything about cookies, I thought. *That's a whole new ball game. Maybe fetching could be fun.*

"Fetch!" ordered Carlotta Bumblecrumb, throwing the ball again.

I ran in front of Mr. Stubble. I got the ball. I returned it.

"Excellent! Good dog!" she said, giving me a cookie.

Mmm, tasty. Fetching isn't so bad, I thought as I chomped. *But what are these two really up to?*

It didn't take long to find out.

OUR FIRST HIT

"Here it is, Mr. Stubble," whispered Carlotta Bumblecrumb. "Thousands of dollars in rare sports junk. Soon it will be ours!"

We peered into the dark window of the

sports collectibles store. Inside were balls, shirts, and photos, all signed by sports stars.

Why are we here? I wondered. *It's bedtime. The store is closed. Besides, these two don't seem like sports fans.*

Carlotta Bumblecrumb opened the store's mail slot. It was exactly the size of a shoebox.

"In you go," she said as Mr. Stubble squeezed me through the slot. "You see? Perfect fit!"

She peeked in at me. "Now fetch the ball!"

I sniffed around. Where was the red ball?

Carlotta Bumblecrumb and Mr. Stubble tapped at the window.

I heard her muffled voice. "Fetch the ball there!" she said. "The one that's signed by Babe Ruth!"

She pointed to a white ball on a stand.

Babe Ruth? I thought. *Wow. This Ruth must be a special babe. Not many babies can sign their names.*

I leaped up to grab the ball with my mouth. *Whoops!* I missed.

I tried again . . . *nope!*

I jumped as high as I could, and crashed to the floor. THUD.

But above me, the stand teetered. The baseball wobbled and fell. It bounced off my head with a *clunk. Ow!* Where did it go?

And what was that loud, terrible sound? It went *WOO WOO WOO WOO*.

The burglar alarm had gone off. But I didn't worry. I didn't know about alarms then. I only knew that I was close to getting a cookie. I had spotted the ball again.

"THERE! GOOD DOG!" Carlotta Bumblecrumb cheered. "Bring it here!"

I pounced on the ball. I chewed it. I rolled it. I chewed it some more. Fetching was so much fun.

"NO, NO, NO!" shouted Carlotta
Bumblecrumb. She looked angry.

What's the matter? I wondered.

A moment later, she peeked into the slot.
She didn't look mad anymore. She held a
cookie out for me.

"Come here with the ball. Nice doggy,"
she said.

I brought the ball to her. *Cookie time!*
Or not.

"Got you, you mangy mutt!" she said, grabbing my collar. She did *not* have the cookie anymore. (I would have smelled it.) She yanked me back through the slot and took the ball.

"It's mine!" she cried, holding it up. "It's mine! It's . . . *covered in doggy drool?* Ew!"

Down the street, police sirens wailed.

"Let's get out of here!"

The limo's tires screeched as we made our getaway.

"Lost them! Hee hee hee," said Carlotta Bumblecrumb. "Mr. Stubble, turn here! We're meeting someone."

He pulled into a dark alley. We stepped out.

A man stood in the shadows. His shoulders twitched. He kept looking back and forth.

"Nervous Ned?" asked Carlotta Bumblecrumb.

"Y-y-y-yes!" said Nervous Ned, jumping in surprise. "How did you know?"

"Just a hunch," she said. "I have the item we discussed. A 1934 baseball signed by Babe Ruth!"

She handed him the ball.

"Nice work, Stumblebum," said Nervous Ned.

"It's *Bumblecrumb!*"

Nervous Ned inspected the ball.

"Wait a minute," he said. "This doesn't say Babe Ruth. It says Blaaghh Rumff."

He pointed to the smudged signature.

Carlotta Bumblecrumb tore the ball from his hands. "It has a little slobber on it, that's all," she said. "This ball is worth a small fortune."

"It's worth something *small* all right," said Nervous Ned. "Like a dime."

Desperately she held me up.

"Then how about an autographed pooch?" she said. "See, her tongue says Babe Ruth, uh . . ."

I stuck out my tongue.

"Backwards," she said.

But Nervous Ned wasn't interested.

CATNAPPING

Our first robbery was a bust. It was back to the warehouse for us. I dozed in my crate while Mr. Stubble read a newspaper. Carlotta Bumblecrumb paced.

"A perfect plan ruined by dog drool!" she said. She pounded the table with her fist. "I had aspirations, you know."

Mr. Stubble looked confused.

"Aspirations, Mr. Stubble!" she said. "Aspirations are things you really want to do. I aspired to be rich. But here I am, wearing cheap plastic jewelry. It's not fair."

Mr. Stubble returned to reading his newspaper. Suddenly he gasped.

"What is it?" she said.

Mr. Stubble pointed to a photo of a fat white cat sitting on a giant can of cat food. Carlotta Bumblecrumb snatched the paper away from him.

"Wagstaff City is proud to welcome Jingles, the famous dancing cat from the Krazy Kitty Cat Food commercials," she read. "He will be staying at our own Come-On-Inn for the next three days."

Back then, the Come-On-Inn didn't allow pets. (How rude!) But Jingles was not your average kitty. He was a VIC, a Very Important Cat.

Carlotta Bumblecrumb's eyes twinkled. "That hip-hopping furball is worth millions! I wish I could get my hands on him."

She cast me a sly look.

"And maybe I can!" she said.

Turns out she had a plan. We tried it the very next day. The *first* part of it worked . . .

NO PETS ALLOWED, warned the Come-On-Inn's sign.

And yet there I was.

But if you were at the inn, you wouldn't have seen me. You'd have seen a lady wearing a room service uniform and plastic jewelry, pushing a cart down a hall. On the cart was a dish topped with a domed food cover.

You wouldn't have seen Mr. Stubble either, but he was there too. He hid under the draping tablecloth. As for me, I was under the food cover on the top of the cart. It was dark under there, but it smelled good.

Mmm, bacon! I thought. *But where is it?*

The cart came to a stop.

"We're at the cat's room," she whispered. "Do we have a surprise for kitty! Hee hee hee."

She knocked on the door.

"Complimentary room service!" she called.

The door creaked open.

"Oh, goody!" said the man who was Jingles's owner. "Please come in."

Carlotta Bumblecrumb rolled the cart across the room.

"Here you are, kitty! A yummy treat just for . . . YOU!" she said, whipping the cover off me.

I blinked in the light.

Inches away from me, Jingles was curled up on a fancy chair. He stared at me in mild surprise.

"MEOW?"

"RUFF?" I responded.

"Go!" my new owner cried. "Chase the cat!
Chase the cat! The—"

Cat? I thought. *But I want bacon!*

I begged on my hind legs. *Bacon, bacon,
PLEASE?*

Carlotta Bumblecrumb groaned.

"Never mind!" she said. "Mr. Stubble,
NOW!"

Mr. Stubble stumbled out from the bottom
of the cart. But he accidentally took the
tablecloth *and me* with him. He looked like
a ghost wearing a dog as a hat.

"Get going!" yelled Carlotta Bumblecrumb. She grabbed the tablecloth to pull it off him. Mr. Stubble tripped and knocked her off her feet. They landed in a heap. The tablecloth had them tied up like a package.

From his chair, Jingles watched us. His eyes narrowed. Then he snarled. This was not good.

Jingles's owner hollered. Furniture crashed. Glass shattered. Finally we all exploded out of the room.

Jingles chased us down the hall and around the inn. Boy, that fat cat could run.

(And that's just *one* reason why cats are not my favorite people.)

A BONEHEADED PLAN

After the Jingles cat-astrophe, we returned to the hideout. Mr. Stubble played jacks. Carlotta Bumblecrumb watched TV. They were supposed to be planning our next move. But they were too sore. They were covered in cat scratches.

Jingles really got them, I thought. And then

there he was again! On TV, he hip-hop danced on a giant can of Krazy Kitty Cat Food.

72

"Bah!" said Carlotta Bumblecrumb. "When I reflect on my life, Mr. Stubble—"

He looked confused, as if he were about to ask a question.

She rolled her eyes. "*Reflecting* means thinking carefully and remembering. When I reflect on my life, I wonder where I went wrong."

She sighed and changed the channel.

"And now," said a TV announcer, "the Museum Network presents *Dinosaurs on Display!*"

"Who cares about a bunch of dusty old bones?" she said.

But Mr. Stubble's eyes lit up, and he pointed at me.

"That's it!" she exclaimed. "We've been going about this all wrong! The pooch should be doing what dogs do naturally. Fetching BONES!"

Something told me fetching bones wasn't going to be as promising as it sounded.

It turns out Carlotta Bumblecrumb had a BIG idea. We were about to commit a dino-size crime.

We waited until night fell. In the moonlight, we crept along the roof of the Museum of Natural History. The skylight on the roof gave us a view into the museum below. Inside was what looked like a giant tower of bones. It was an all-you-can-chew bone buffet!

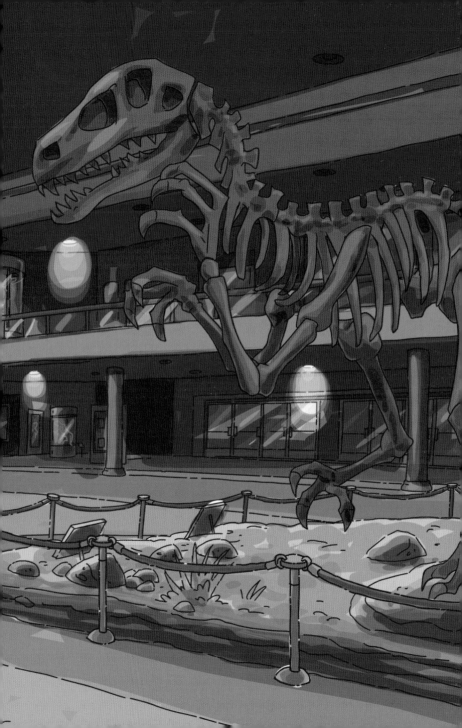

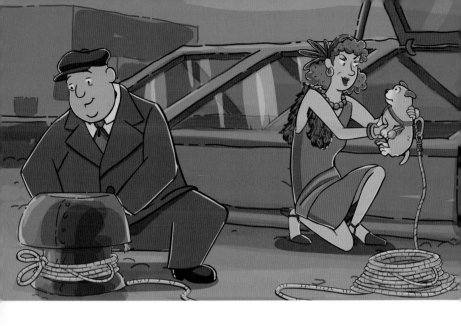

"There it is, the T. rex!" said Carlotta Bumblecrumb. "I'm done reminiscing, Mr. Stubble. No more thinking and talking about the past. The past is about to make us rich! We'll steal that dinosaur, even if we have to do it one bone at a time."

Mr. Stubble pried the window open.

"Okay, pooch," she said. "Your job is very simple. Fetch the bones. Got it?"

I nodded. *My pleasure!*

Mr. Stubble tied a rope around me. He tied the other end to a ventilation pipe. Then he slipped me through the open window. I dropped lower and lower, until . . . I stopped in midair.

"We're caught in the rope, Mr. Stubble!" I heard Carlotta Bumblecrumb yell from above. "Turn this way! Lift your leg. NO! Other leg!"

Meanwhile I was swinging around like a yo-yo on a string.

"Turn around, you clumsy—argh! WAIT! I'll do it!"

Finally, I was lowered to the museum floor. I had been looking forward to the bone buffet, but as soon as my paws hit the ground, I lost my appetite. I longed to go back up to the roof.

That T. rex looked a million times bigger from the ground. Its jaws were open. Its teeth were huge. And it looked like it hadn't eaten for a long *long* time.

Gulp! *I'm about to be a dino snack,* I thought.

BUSTING BUFFOONS

"It's just a bunch of bones!" Carlotta
Bumblecrumb called down. "Fetch them!"

Slooooowly, I crept over to the dinosaur. I
concentrated on the foot, not the mouth. Up
close, it didn't look so scary. It looked kind of
. . . *delicious*.

I chomped down on a toe. Grrr. I tugged
and tugged, until SNAP! The bone broke off.

But then there was a loud *creak!* And a
frightening *crack!* And—uh-oh! The whole
T. rex was breaking apart. Bones crashed to
the floor.

Before my eyes, the T. rex was turning
into a huge cloud of dust. Then I heard more
loud noises.

WOO WOO WOO WOO
the burglar alarm went
off. And up above, Carlotta
Bumblecrumb and Mr. Stubble
shrieked.

I ran to hide.

When the dust settled, I
saw that my rope had wrapped
around their ankles. It had
dragged them through the
roof's open window.
And now they
dangled upside
down, swinging
back and forth.
Their noses just
missed the pile of
bones.

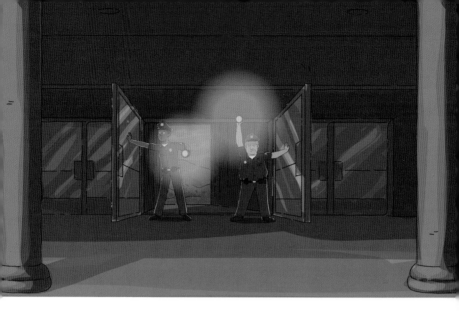

"Get me down!" yelled Carlotta
Bumblecrumb.

I heard a thumping sound and some groans.

Soon I heard police sirens outside the
museum. From my hiding spot, I saw two
cops rush in. They swept their flashlights
across the room.

"What in the world is going on?" said one
police officer.

Their lights stopped at the pile of bones.

The T. rex skull rocked as if it were nodding.

"It's alive!" shouted the other policeman.

No, it was just little old me. I popped up from inside the skull and ran over to the police.

Carlotta Bumblecrumb and Mr. Stubble were nowhere in sight. But I knew they were there. Dogs have great noses.

"WOOF!" I barked. And then I let my great dog nose lead us all to a display of two cave people. "Woof!" I said again, which meant "Check out these buffoons!"—in Dog of course.

One officer took a good look.

"There's something odd about these cave people," he said.

He patted the cave man's fur vest. Dust flew into the air.

"Ah-ah-ah . . . choo!" Mr. Stubble sneezed.

Carlotta Bumblecrumb groaned.

Mr. Stubble spoke. "Oops," he said. "Sorry Ms. Bumblecrumb."

"Okay, boneheads," said the policeman. "You're under arrest."

"Move it, Dumblebum," his partner said.

"It's BUMBLECRUMB!" she yelled. "Can't anyone get it right?"

One cop hauled the crooks away.

The other patted my head. "Sorry, girl. We have to take you to the animal shelter."

After my recent adventures, that didn't seem so bad.

TA-DA!

The next morning, Helen was in her kitchen. She was reluctantly looking at photos of cats.

"What about this one?" asked Mom. At the kitchen table, she held up a cute image of a kitten. "She's the same color as Martha."

"I guess."

"You could name her Martha," said Mom.

Helen walked to the fridge. She took down a drawing of me. "You think we could train her to fetch?"

Mom frowned. "Well . . ."

Just then, Dad burst in.

"Hey, can you guys give me a hand with the groceries?" he asked.

"Groceries?" said Mom. "But we went shopping yesterday."

"Don't you recall?" said Dad. "I said I might go *by there* on the way home from work?"

He winked.

"Ah!" said Mom. "On the way home from work! That's terrific!"

What's so terrific about groceries? Helen
wondered.

"I'll need help from you two," said Dad.

"Sure," said Mom.

"Okay," mumbled Helen. She looked at her
drawing one last time. Then she dropped it
into the trash.

Helen shuffled outside after her parents. In the driveway, she peeked into Dad's car.

"There aren't any groceries," she said, confused.

That's when I popped up from the back seat. TA-DA! I'd been waiting there to surprise her.

"Martha!" Helen cried. "You got Martha!"

She opened the car door. She wrapped me up in a hug. I gave her cheek a slobbery kiss.

"Whee!" shouted Helen, spinning me around. "Martha, you're home at last!"

And it was true. I was home.

HOME SWEET HOME

When Martha was done talking, the sun had begun to set over the duck pond.

Truman put his pen down.

"Wow," he said. "I can't believe what I've just heard."

"Sorry," said Martha. "That was my stomach. I'm hungry."

"Not that. I'm talking about your interesting background."

Martha looked at her back. "They are nice spots," she said.

"No," said Truman. "Your background is all the things that have happened to you in your past," he explained. "What a life story! In the end, all your aspirations came true."

"That's right," Martha said. "It was everything I ever could have hoped for."

"Me, too," said a voice behind her.

Martha turned to see the little red-haired girl. Only she wasn't so little anymore. Just like Martha was no longer a puppy.

"Helen!" cried Martha.

Helen gave her a big hug. Martha licked Helen's cheek.

"If your autobiography is done, dinner is waiting," said Helen.

"Dinner? Yes!" said Martha. "Race you!"

"You bet!" shouted Helen.

"Wait for me!" yelled Truman.

And they all ran home sweet home.

Martha Speaks
GLOSSARY

H ow many words do you remember from the story?

aspiration: something a person really wants to do

autobiography: the story of a person's life told in that person's own words

background: all the things that happened in the past

flashback: scene in a book, play, movie, or TV program that shows something that happened earlier

narrate: to tell a story

possibility: something that can happen

promising: likely to work out just right

reminisce: to think or talk about things that happened in the past

sequence: order of actions according to when they happen

yearn: to really want

AUTOBIOGRAPHY

Staple a few sheets of notebook paper down the left side to create your own book. Martha and Truman wrote a few sentences to help you get started.

[your name] 's Amazing Life Story
An Interesting Background

My life story is doggone amazing!

My name is [fill in your name here]. I was born on [birthday] in [city, state]. [Tell funny or interesting story about you as a baby here.]

I have [number] people in my family. They are [names of family members].

I have [number] pets in my family. They include [names and types of pets].

Today I am [age] years old. I am in the [grade] grade at [school]. I live in [city, state]. My friends are [names].

When we're together, we like to [list of favorite activities].

YOU fill in the rest.

My future is full of promising possibilities. The rest of my life story should be doggone amazing, too!

Martha Says, "Say Cheese!"

Martha has left this empty frame for you. Draw or trace the frame six times on blank sheets of paper. Then draw or paste pictures of yourself at different ages and label them (me as a baby, first day of school, now, future) to illustrate your autobiography. You can even cut and paste the pictures in a different sequence to create flashbacks!

Shelter Dog Blues

Adaptation by Jamie White
Based on a TV series teleplay written by Matt Steinglass
Based on the characters created by Susan Meddaugh

MARTHA
SAYS HELLO

Hi there!

It's me, Martha, here
to introduce my story.

If I were any other dog,
my introduction might go
something like this:

Woof. Woof, woof.

But ever since Helen fed
me her alphabet soup, I've
been a dog who can speak.
And speak and speak . . .

No one's sure how or why, but the letters in the soup traveled up to my brain instead of down to my stomach.

Now, as long as I eat my daily bowl of alphabet soup, I can talk. To my family: Helen, baby Jake, Mom, Dad, and our dog Skits, who only speaks Dog. To Helen's best friend, T.D. To anyone who'll listen.

Sometimes my family wishes I didn't talk *quite* so much. But who would want to discourage a talking dog from, well, talking?

Besides, my speaking comes in handy. One night, I called 911 to stop a burglar.

So I guess I'm fortunate. Lucky, that is. But you never know when you might go from lucky to *unlucky*. Last week I found out what it's like to be unlucky and lose the most precious thing of all—freedom.

Sit, stay, and hear all about it . . .

A BUBBLE-NOSED DOG

It all started in the bathroom.

Martha could think of only one good reason to visit the bathroom: to drink from the toilet. But sometimes Martha was dragged to the bathroom against her will.

"You have no right!" Martha yelled, squirming in Helen's arms. "It's not fair!"

"You *have* to take a bath," Helen said. "Get in there!"

Helen began to drop Martha into the soapy water.

"No!" Martha cried. "Not the bubbles! Anything but the—"

SPLASH!

"Bubbles," Martha groaned. She was soaked. "I HATE bubbles! They get in my mouth!"

"If you *ever* stopped talking, that wouldn't happen," Helen said.

"They get up my nose too. Look!" Martha snorted two bubbles into the air.

"Martha, you're fortunate to have a family that gives you a bath when you need one," Helen said.

"Having to do something you hate

108

doesn't seem very *fortunate* to me," Martha
replied.

"If you knew how many dogs are all alone
in the world, you'd appreciate how lucky you
are."

Helen snapped off Martha's collar. She
hung it on the shower rod so she could scrub
Martha's neck. Outside, a truck rumbled.

"Helen!" Mom called from downstairs. "Did you take out the garbage yet? I hear the truck coming!"

"Be right there!" Helen said. "Lucky dog," she said to Martha. "Just a quick bath today."

Hooray for garbage trucks, Martha thought. She leaped out of the tub.

"So are you fortunate to have to take out the garbage?" Martha asked as Helen dried her off.

"No, but Mom is fortunate she has me to take it out for her," Helen said. "I'd better go."

As soon as Helen left, Martha felt strange. Something was missing, she thought. She looked up at the shower rod.

"Wait," Martha said. "You forgot my collar!"

"I'll get it later!" Helen called.

Humans, Martha thought. *If a dog wants something done right, she has to do it herself.*

Martha jumped onto the edge of the tub and reached for her collar. The tub was slippery. Her paws slid—and *oof!* Martha fell onto her belly.

"It's times like these I wish I had hands," Martha said.

She leaped back onto the tub. But her paws refused to stay put. Martha slipped again.

"ACK!" she cried, grabbing the shower curtain.

This time, Martha took the curtain and rod down with her. They all crashed into the tub.

When Martha's head popped out of the water, she looked like she'd grown a bubble beard. She eyed what had fallen onto the soap dish.

"My collar!" Martha said, grabbing for it. "Whoops!"

Her paw hit the edge of the dish. The collar shot through the air and landed on the windowsill.

"Phew," said Martha. "Safe and sound."

And that's when her collar slid right out the window.

THE DOGGONE DAY BLUES

"NOOOOOO!" Martha cried, looking out the window.

Her collar was in the trash can below. It had fallen on top of a banana peel and a half-eaten hot dog.

Hot dog—yum! Martha thought. *Wait, I can't think about food at a time like this. I have to get that trash can!*

"I WANT THAT GARBAGE! DON'T LET
THEM TAKE IT!" Martha cried. She raced
downstairs.

By the time she got outside, the trash man
was already dumping the garbage into his
truck. He handed the empty can back to Helen.

"GIVE ME THAT TRASH!" Martha yelled.

The truck began to pull away.

"Martha!" said Helen. "Why are you all wet
again?"

"No time for chitchat," Martha said.

Helen and Mom watched Martha chase the truck down the street.

"No time to talk?" Helen said. "What's gotten into Martha?"

Mom shook her head. "Chasing after garbage trucks! That dog is acting like a . . . dog! Next thing you know, she'll be drinking from the toilet."

. . . . .

As Helen and Mom watched Martha disappear,
the trash man watched Martha grow closer.
Covered in bubbles, she was a scary sight. The
trash man called Animal Rescue.

"Officer Kazuo here," said the voice at the
other end. "Can I help you?"

Kazuo was driving the Shelter Mobile. *BUM,
BUM, BADUM* went the radio. People could
hear him coming from blocks away.

"An out-of-control dog?"
Kazuo said. *"Chasing you?*
Covered in *foam?* Stay away
from that dog. I'll be right
there!"

Kazuo slammed his foot on the gas. A dog that was foaming at the mouth could have rabies! The Shelter Mobile sped down the street.

Meanwhile, the garbage truck stopped to pick up a dumpster. Martha caught up to it.

"Hold on! My collar is in there!" she yelled. But her voice could not be heard over the sound of the garbage truck.

Why won't he listen to me? Martha wondered. *I'm a talking dog, for crying out loud. If only I could speak to him face to face . . .*

She leaped to his window.

The trash collector still couldn't hear
Martha. But he *could* see a crazy-looking dog
pop up and down.

"Oh, golly!" he yelled, locking his door.

"Collie? No, I'm looking for my *collar!*
That's the thing that goes around my *neck,*"
Martha said.

The Shelter Mobile screeched to a halt next
to her.

"Let's rock and roll," Kazuo said, hopping out. He put on his headphones and crept toward Martha. He held a long stick with a loop at its end.

Oh, good, thought Martha. *Someone to help me.*

"Could you explain to him that I'm searching for my collar?" she asked.

Kazuo walked closer. With his headphones on, he couldn't hear a word Martha said.

"Doesn't *anybody* here understand Human?" said Martha. "Hey, what's that stick thing for?"

Kazuo lowered his catch pole.

"Gotcha!" he said.

Before she knew it, Martha was locked in the back of the Shelter Mobile.

She was alone, with no one to hear her. *In this situation, there is only one thing for a dog to do,* she thought.

Martha sang the doggone day blues.

THE DOGGY SLAMMER

It was a sad, lonely ride to the animal shelter. It was also a long time for Martha to go without talking. It was the first thing she did when Kazuo took her out of the Shelter Mobile.

"You don't understand! My collar is lost in the garbage," Martha tried to explain.

It was no use. Kazuo was still wearing his headphones. *BUM, BUM, BADUM,* he hummed.

He carried her to the back of the pound's reception area. He pressed a button on the wall.

BZZZZ.

A door opened to a room full of cages. Dogs of all shapes and sizes barked at them.

"In you go!" said Kazuo, shepherding her into a cage.

Martha looked around her small cell. The only things in it were an old chew toy and a bowl of dry dog food.

"What, no burgers?" Martha said. "No chops? Not even a lousy meatball? Maybe I can order in?"

Kazuo left.

"Wait!" Martha cried. "I don't belong here! This is all a big mistake! I *have* a family!"

In the cage next to her, an old bulldog barked. *Ruff, ruff!*

"What do you mean, 'That's what they all say'?" Martha asked.

· · · · ·

At home, Helen was worried. She hadn't seen
Martha in hours.

"Don't fret," Mom said. "She's been gone
longer than this before."

"She'll be back when she's hungry," said
Dad. "Martha never misses a meal."

"You don't think she feels neglected,
do you?" Helen asked.

"Neglected? *Martha?*" Dad said. "How
could she? Neglected dogs are dogs who are
forgotten or ignored. You
take good care of Martha.
You wash her, you
groom her—"

"WASH?" Helen cried.

"Oh, no! I just realized something. I never put Martha's collar back on after her bath. She's not wearing her tags!"

"Oh, dear," Mom said. "Let's call the animal shelter."

Dad ran to the phone.

Kazuo was locking up for the night when he heard the telephone ring.

He picked it up and said, "Hello. This is the Animal Rescue Shelter. We're about to close."

"Could you tell me if you picked up a talking dog today?" Dad asked.

"Sir, I can't check the records now, but—" Kazuo narrowed his eyes. "Did you say a *talking* dog?"

"Yes," said Dad. "A dog that can speak. Human language."

"Sir, is this some type of joke?" Kazuo asked.

"Of course not. I'm looking for a talking—"

Click. The phone went dead.

"I guess that's a *no,* then," said Dad.

MARTHA'S SIDE OF THE STORY

So there I was, in the pound. The pooch hooch. The doggy basket of steel.

The place was full of tough dogs who looked like they'd just as soon bite me as sniff me. There was Estelle, the grizzled old poodle;

Wally, the pointer with the chewed-up ear; and Miranda, the cutest Yorkie-poodle you ever saw. (Okay, maybe they weren't *all* so tough.)

Someone growled in the cage next to mine. It was Pops, the bulldog. He was the toughest of them all.

"Sorry, is there a problem?" I asked.

Pops glared at me.

"I'll only be here a day or two," I gulped. "I don't mean to cause any—"

RAAARR! RUFF!

"Oh. My name? I'm Martha," I said. "What's yours?"

"Pops," he barked.

"What are you in for?" I asked.

Pops told me his story. It was rough. He was once a junkyard dog. Pops protected his master's yard like a one-dog burglar alarm.

But then his master sold the junkyard, bought a flashy car, and sped off. Poor old Pops was left in the dust. Then there was Miranda in a nearby cage. Her story was sad too. She lived with a rich lady in a big house. She was a good dog. She barked politely. She obeyed every command. Her golden fur perfectly matched the golden colors of the lady's living room. Until the lady changed the room to blue, that is.

"Honey, you don't match the drapes," the lady said one day. And Miranda was tossed into a limo for a one-way ride to Poundsville.

Every dog here was abandoned and alone. Estelle's owners moved to a building where no pets were allowed. And the puppies—Streak, Butterscotch, and Mandarin—never had an owner at all. Or at least they had been brought to the shelter before they could remember.

"I know how you feel," I told them.

Ruff! Ruff! barked Pops.

"What a harsh thing to say," I replied. "Of course I've had it rough. Why, just today, I had to take a . . . *bath!*"

The dogs rolled their eyes.

"With *bubbles!*" I said. "They get in your nose!"

Pops growled.

"Sure, my family will get me in the morning. But I know what it's like to feel unloved," I said. "I was in the shelter when I was a puppy. That's where Helen found me."

They had stopped listening. They had turned their backs. I needed to do something—fast.

"What if I told you I could get us all out of this place?" I said. "Together."

The dogs barked in excitement. Even Pops looked interested.

"Leave it to me," I said. "I have a plan!"

Okay, I thought. *Time to come up with a plan.*

BREAKING AND EXITING

Martha's plan to break out of the shelter had three simple steps:

Step one: Pick up a piece of dog food.

Step two: Flick it at the door's access button.

Step three: If steps one and two don't work, try them again.

Martha didn't really expect to need step three. But she did. She flicked dog food at the button for hours.

The dogs watched pellet after pellet fly by. Some pellets hit the door. Some hit the wall. But even when they hit the button, the door didn't open. Finally, the dogs fell asleep. The only one left watching was a pigeon perched on a cage. And he just shook his head and rolled his eyes.

If I could just figure out how to make something heavier fly across the room, Martha said to herself.

Then she remembered what had started
this whole mess. *My collar flew into the air when
I hit the soap dish,* she thought. *Aha!*

Martha rested the chew toy on her bowl.
She slid the bowl out through the bars of
her cage. Then she slammed her paw onto the
bowl. The chewie whizzed across the room.

Bull's-eye! The door opened with a buzz.

"I DID IT! WE'RE OUT!" Martha cheered,
looking around at the dogs. "We're out!
We're, uh . . ."

The dogs yawned.

"There must be something I've
overlooked," Martha said. "What did I
forget?"

Ruff, ruff! Pops barked.

"Er, right," Martha mumbled. "I forgot that
we're all inside locked cages."

Martha rattled her door.

"Hey, pigeon!" she called. "Can I get your
help down here?"

Coo, coo, said the pigeon.

"What's in it for you?" Martha repeated. "No wonder they call you flying rats!"

The pigeon turned away.

"Wait!" Martha said. "My neighbors keep a twenty-pound bag of birdseed in their garage. You get me out, I'll get you in."

The pigeon swooped down to
Martha's cage. It pushed the door's unlock
button with its head. *Click.* The door
swung open.

"Yippee!" Martha said. "I'm free!"

Martha hurried to open the other cages.
A happy pack of dogs ran into the reception
area. Everyone raced for the exit.

"Now all we have to do is open this last
door," Martha said. "Then we'll be as
free as—*Kazuo?!*"

The dogs skidded to a halt.

"Negative," Kazuo said, walking in with
a phone to his ear. "Dog escape is under
control. Repeat, dog escape is under control!"

"Well, this is unfortunate timing,"
Martha said.

Near her, Pops growled.

Pops is so close to freedom, he can smell it,
Martha thought. *Or maybe he smells the Burger
Barn down the street. Mmm, burgers . . . Uh-oh!
Where is Pops going?*

Pops ran under Kazuo's legs and out
the door.

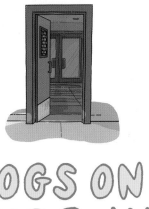

DOGS ON THE RUN

"Hey, Pops! Get back here!" Kazuo called.

Pops was on the run.

So was Martha. She ran out the door, past Kazuo, and down the street. Pops was faster than he looked, but it didn't take her long to catch up with him.

"Stop, Pops! What about the others?" she said.

Suddenly, she heard a *BUM, BUM, BADUM!* Headlights beamed on them from behind.

"Watch out!" Martha said to Pops. "The Shelter Mobile is on our tails!"

"You'll never make it, Pops!" Kazuo shouted.

Pops and Martha raced around a corner.

"This is a dead-end street," Martha said. "Up ahead! He can't follow us there!"

The dogs fled into the woods.

Behind them, the Shelter Mobile screeched to a stop. Kazuo got out to chase them on foot.

"Pops! We're leaving the others behind!" Martha said. She stopped to catch her breath. "How can we enjoy being free when we deserted them—"

Before Martha could finish, she felt something familiar around her neck. And it wasn't her collar.

"Gotcha again!" Kazuo said, holding the catch pole.

"Please," Martha said. "Let Pops go! I can explain—"

"That's enough from you," Kazuo

"You finally hear me?" Martha asked. "I was beginning to wonder if you could only hear music. Or if you had ears. Or if—"

151

"Shhh. Did I ask for your opinion?"
Kazuo said. He looked up to see Pops in
the distance. "Pops, what are you doing?"

The old bulldog stood in the moonlight.

"We've been through this before," Kazuo
said softly. "You break out, the world is harsh,
and you feel neglected. Three weeks later,
you're at the shelter again. Come back, Pops.
We'll find you a family."

Pops hung his head. He shuffled
toward Kazuo.

"Nice dog," said Kazuo.

Martha watched as Kazuo scratched
Pops's head.

Kazuo might not have good ears, Martha
thought, *but he has a good heart.*

A NEW DAY

When Martha saw her shelter friends again, it was from behind bars.

Everyone is sad about being back in a cage, Martha thought. *It's all my fault.*

The dogs sulked in silence. The only sound came from the pigeon.

Coo, coo.

"Yes, the birdseed deal is still on!" Martha snapped. "Jeepers."

Kazuo came in carrying bags of dog food.

"Howdy, boys and girls," he chirped. "Why the long faces? It's morning. Say hello to a new day!"

Nobody answered.

"Or not," Kazuo said. "Listen, I know this place can get gloomy. But I'm trying to find you families. Escaping doesn't help anybody. Why don't we make a fresh start?"

He turned to Martha. "Hey, new dog! What kind of chow do you like? Bark once for Meaty Bix, twice for Waggy Wafers."

"My name is Martha," she said. "And I'd like Meaty Bix, please!"

"Let's try this again," said Kazuo. "Bark once for Meaty Bix, twice for Waggy Wafers."

"I don't need to bark. I can talk! Can't I just phone my family so they can bring me home?" Martha asked.

"I'm sorry. Dogs are not allowed to make phone calls," Kazuo replied.

"But you said you hoped we'd find families," Martha said. "I already have one."

"Kid, you have no collar to prove you belong to anyone. If I let you use the phone, then all the dogs will want to."

"Well, didn't anyone call here looking for me?" Martha asked.

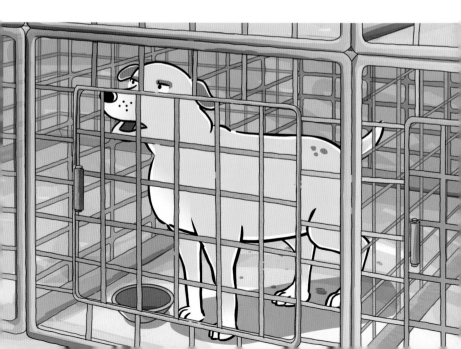

"Oh, yeah. Somebody did call," Kazuo
said, scratching his head. "About a talking dog.
But how do I know you're *that* talking dog?"

"Kazuo!" Martha said.

He sighed. "Okay. What's your number?"

Martha told him. Kazuo began to dial.

"Wait," he said. "What if you're just calling
another talking dog?"

Martha groaned. "Someone is acting like a birdbrain in this room, and it's NOT the pigeon."

"Oh, all right." Kazuo held the phone to Martha's ear.

"Hello?" Helen answered.

"It's me!" Martha said, wagging her tail. "I'm in the animal shelter."

"Martha! Thank goodness! Are you all right?" Helen asked.

"Yes," said Martha.

"That's terrific. I'm so happy," Helen said. "May I ask you something?"

"Sure. What's that?" said Martha.

"WHAT WERE YOU THINKING?" Helen shouted. "WHY DID YOU CHASE STINKY GARBAGE? DO YOU HAVE ANY IDEA HOW WORRIED WE'VE BEEN?"

"Wow," Kazuo said. "Anyone who cares enough to yell that loud has got to be your family."

MARTHA SPEAKS AGAIN

And that's how I busted out of doggy jail.
Kazuo and I waited for my family in the
reception area. It was hard to sit still.

"You have ants in your pants," Kazuo said.

"Kazuo! Dogs do not wear pants," I said.
"Well, unless you count my terrier friend,
Frank. Now, that's just embarrassing.

I mean—"

"Okay, okay," Kazuo said. "Your family will be here soon, Martha. We'll miss you."

"I'll miss you all too. I want to take everyone home with me," I said. "Why is it so hard to find families for the dogs?"

"I guess people don't know about them," Kazuo said.

"I wish we could show everybody how great these dogs are," I said.

Just then, two of my favorite people burst through the door.

"MARTHA!" Helen shouted.

I leaped into Helen's arms. It felt great to be hugged again.

"Thanks for finding our Martha," Mom said to Kazuo. "It will be nice to get her home."

"Oh, I'm not leaving," I said.

"What?" said Helen.

"I've decided I can't abandon my friends. Come meet them!"

I introduced Helen and Mom to the others. The dogs all looked so sad.

"Maybe we could adopt them," Helen said. "They could be part of our family."

Mom shook her head. "That's a lot of dogs."

"And a lot of responsibility," said Kazuo. "I couldn't let you adopt them all unless I knew you could take care of each and every one."

For the first time in my life, I couldn't find any words. At least none that were encouraging.

"How can we get people to adopt the dogs?" Helen asked me as we walked out into the shelter yard.

"They just have to meet them," I said. "Maybe we can sneak the dogs into houses at night. Then when the people wake up—

bingo! They have a dog. It's like Christmas."

"But what if they don't make good families?" Helen said. "Like Kazuo said, people have to want the dogs."

"Right," I said, thinking again.

The faint sound of music interrupted my thoughts. It was the theme song to my favorite TV talent show.

"Hey, we're missing *International Icon*," I said.

"Who cares?" Helen said.

"Only everybody," I said. I call to vote for my favorite contestant every week. "Who can resist great talent?"

Helen's face lit up.

"A dog talent show!" we said together.

It was a great idea, if I do say so myself.

"We can have it right here at the shelter tomorrow," I said. "You spread the word. I'll get the dogs ready. I can't wait to see the looks on their faces when I tell them!"

I told the dogs our idea and waited for their applause. And waited . . .

This was not the reaction I had imagined— no reaction.

"Just give it a shot," I said. "I can't promise anything. But with everyone's help, we can make this show a success. It's not going to be easy. It's going to be work, work, and more work. But you can do it!"

The dogs stood a little straighter. They were listening, and I didn't have to offer any of them a single doggy treat.

"You're going out there dogs," I said, "and you're coming back . . . Well, you'll still be dogs. But YOU'LL HAVE FAMILIES!"

The dogs barked cheerily.

Except for one. Pops grunted and went back to sleep.

BEST PAW FORWARD

Helen and her best friend, T.D., delivered flyers to every dogless kid in town.

They went to all kinds of houses—small, big, neat, and messy. They visited a noisy house of triplets who didn't like to share. And the quiet apartment of a boy who traveled a lot.

"Come see Wagstaff City's Top Dog," Helen said to the boy. "It's the best dog show ever."

"If you're lucky, you'll take home a pet of your own," T.D. added.

The boy frowned. "My parents say it'd be too hard to take a dog on a plane with us."

It seemed like everyone had an excuse for not getting a dog. But Helen and T.D. promised them a show they'd never forget.

· · · · ·

Back at the shelter, Martha was giving the dogs their first lesson in being irresistible.

"Put your best paw forward," she told them. "Let's show the people what makes you, you. Streak, Butterscotch, and Mandarin, what do you do best?"

The puppies stared blankly. They were young and didn't understand Martha's instructions.

"You're affectionate. Show me!"

Yip, yip, yip! they all yipped together.

"QUIET!" Martha said. "Loud yipping is not being affectionate."

Yap? Streak asked.

"Being affectionate means being friendly and showing people you love them," Martha answered. "You know how to do that, right?"

The puppies pounced on Martha and covered her with kisses.

"Okay! A little less affection . . . and drool," Martha said.

Martha turned to Wally, the pointer. "Show me your best quality, Wally!"

He ran to a puddle.

What kind of talent do we have here? Martha wondered.

Wally dropped and rolled. He was a muddy mess. Then he trotted back and shook his coat. Mud splattered onto everyone.

"Maybe we need to review what I meant
when I said best quality," said Martha, shaking
herself off. "No one comes to the shelter
saying, 'Give me your dirtiest dog.' People
want clean. They want cute. They want . . .
the low wiggle."

The dogs looked confused.

"You don't know what the low wiggle
is?" Martha said. "It works like this. When
someone comes into the shelter—POW! You
turn on the charm. Watch me."

Martha smiled and wagged her tail.

"This is how to say, 'I like you! I hope you like me.' Then you crouch low to the ground and wiggle toward the person. See?" Martha wiggled with her rear in the air.

"For the big finish, show your belly!" Martha flopped onto her back. "Now you try."

The dogs ran in circles. Some crashed into each other. A few skipped the wiggle and went straight for the belly move.

"This is going to take a lot of work," Martha muttered. She looked at Pops, alone in the corner. "Pops, how about you?"

Pops just walked away.

Maybe you can't teach an old dog new tricks, Martha thought. *But I will try. I'll get this ragtag bunch ready for tomorrow's show if it takes me all day.*

Sure enough, Martha was still talking after the sun set. "Eyes, ears, and tails! Come on! I want to see wagging!"

It was a long night.

TOP DOG

The next day, the dogs couldn't believe how many people had come to see them.

"Look at this crowd!" Helen said. "We're sure to get the dogs adopted."

"Don't get your hopes too high," Dad said. "Kazuo has been trying for a long time."

At last, the show was about to begin.

Martha made her grand entrance.

"Welcome to Wagstaff City's Top Dog! I'm your host, Martha. It's time for this show to go to the dogs!"

The dogs strutted down the stage as if it were a runway.

"Awwww!" said the crowd, enjoying the show already.

"Do you want a dog who is always your friend no matter what?" Martha said. "Well, dogs don't come any more loyal than Wally!"

Wally came out wearing his most
loyal look.

"He is so loyal, he nearly lost an ear
protecting his last owner from a bear!"

Wally showed off his chewed-up ear. The
crowd gasped.

"Is that true?" T.D. asked Helen.

"Mostly," Helen said, "NOT."

"I know we travel a lot, but could we *please*
adopt him, Dad?" asked a boy.

"I don't know," said the boy's dad. "How would we take him with us?"

"*Psst,* Wally," Helen whispered. She held an animal carrier. Wally marched inside and shut the door behind him.

"A frequent flyer dog for the family on the go!" Helen said.

"That's the dog for us!" said the boy's dad.

"YES!" said the boy, hugging his father.

Then Estelle pranced onto the stage.

"She's elegant! She's stylish! But is she devoted?" Martha said, looking at a girl in the audience.

"If *devoted* means someone who's going to love you forever, then that's Estelle!"

Estelle did a perfect low wiggle.

"And a poodle won't get hair on your chair," Martha said to the girl's mom.

The mom nodded to her daughter.

"Woo-hoo!" cheered the girl. Estelle leaped into her arms.

Butterscotch trotted out next. She nuzzled Martha's leg.

"What does every human dream of in a dog?" Martha said. "Affection! As you can see, Butterscotch is the most affectionate— HEY!"

One of the triplets yanked Butterscotch off the stage.

"You're mine," she said, kissing the puppy's ear.

"She's mine!" yelled her sister.

"No, mine!" yelled the other.

"Please stop fighting! There's more where she came from," Martha said.

Streak and Mandarin came out. The girls scooped them up.

"We're so happy," the triplets said, holding their new pets.

"Me too," said their dad, holding his head.

By the end of the show, each dog had found a family. Or so Martha thought.

"Thanks for coming," she said. "You'll find adoption forms in—"

"Martha, you forgot someone," Helen whispered loudly. She pointed to the stage steps, where Pops sat alone.

"Oops," said Martha. "Pops, do you want to come up here too?"

Pops snuffled, hesitating.

"We have one last contestant," Martha told the crowd. "Give a big paw . . . I mean *hand* for Pops!"

Pops advanced onto the stage.

"Pops may look fierce, but he's as loyal and affectionate as any dog here. Would anyone like to take him home?" Martha asked as the people stood to leave.

"Anyone?" she asked again. But everyone was heading toward the door.

Poor Pops, Martha thought. *He'll feel lonelier than ever.*

Pops began to walk off the stage when a voice stopped him.

"*I'll* adopt him," someone said.

Martha spun around. "Kazuo?"

"Pops, you and I go back a long time," said Kazuo. "What do you say, old guy? Will you be my dog?"

Pops scowled.

Come on, Pops, Martha thought. *Say yes.*

Pops's grumpy face broke into a huge smile. He licked Kazuo's cheek. "Hooray!" the remaining crowd cheered.

"Sealed with a slobbery kiss!" Martha said. "It looks like my work here is done."

MARTHA SAYS GOODBYE

Well, that's my story.

My shelter friends love their new families. Kazuo is still hosting talent shows. I hear Pops is even introducing the low wiggle to new dogs. I guess you *can* teach an old dog new tricks!

As for me, I went from being lucky to *unlucky* back to lucky again.

196

Now I'm the same fortunate dog I used to be. *Un*fortunately, I've ended up in the same place where this story began. The bathroom.

Still, it's good to be home with my chewies, soup, and most of all, family. Yes, I love everything about my home.

Well, almost everything . . . I still HATE baths.

Uh-oh. I see bubbles. Time to *gooooooooooooooooooo!*

GLOSSARY

How many words do you remember from the story?

abandon: to leave behind or give up

adopt: to make someone a part of one's family

adore: to love and admire

affectionate: friendly, loving

deserted: left behind or given up by others

devoted: dedicated, loyal

fortunate: lucky in life

loyal: faithful to someone no matter what

neglected: not cared for properly, forgotten

overlooked: forgotten, missed, or ignored

unfortunate: unlucky

A story by Martha, illustrated by T.D.

The Deserted Hot Dog

> Help Martha write her story! Fill in the
> blanks with the new words you've learned.

Once upon a time, there was a little hot dog.

It sat on the grill getting nice and warm

with all its hot dog friends.

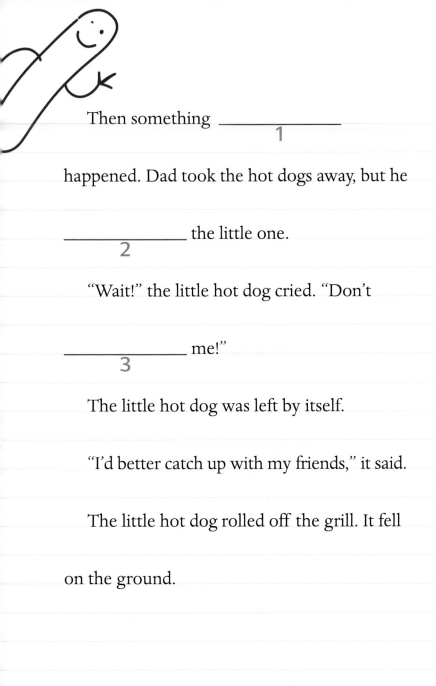

Then something _____
1

happened. Dad took the hot dogs away, but he

_____ the little one.
2

"Wait!" the little hot dog cried. "Don't

_____ me!"
3

The little hot dog was left by itself.

"I'd better catch up with my friends," it said.

The little hot dog rolled off the grill. It fell

on the ground.

"Oof!" it said. "I'm _____ and
4

alone. What will I do?"

Just then, something _____
5

happened. Martha appeared.

Martha had never _____ a hot
6

dog in her life.

"I _____ hot dogs," she said.
7

"I am their most _____ and
8

_____ fan. When I was a puppy at
9

the shelter, I dreamed a hot dog seller would

_____ me. Then I'd eat hot dogs
10

all day."

Martha ate every hot dog, even the little

one. It traveled into her stomach, where it

joined the others.

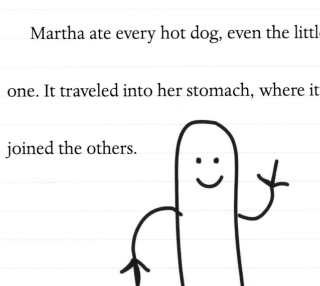

"Woo-hoo!" the hot dog friends cheered.

Being _____ hot dogs, they
11

hugged each other. Then they had a party.

The moral of the story is, if you are a

lonely, deserted hot dog, come see Martha!

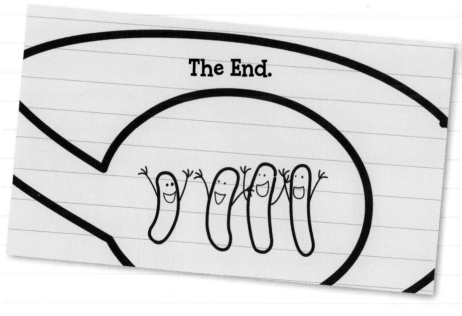

Answers

1 unfortunate
2 overlooked
3 abandon
4 deserted
5 fortunate
6 neglected
7 adore
8 loyal or devoted
9 loyal or devoted
10 adopt
11 affectionate

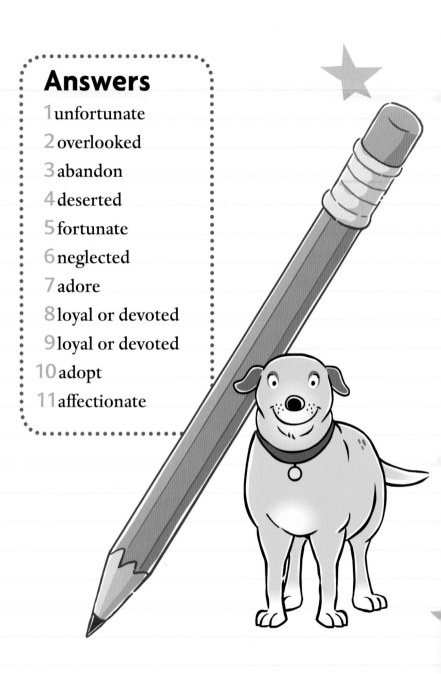

Add up your correct answers.
Then read what Martha says:

If you have . . .

9–11 correct answers, you are a TOP DOG.
"Congratulations! Way to put your best paw forward!"

6–8 correct answers, you are a HOT DOG.
"Nice job! With a little more work, you're sure to get them all right!"

0–5 correct answers, you are a POUND PUP.
"Like the dogs at the shelter learned, practice makes perfect. Keep trying—and you'll soon be top dog!"

Martha's
Silly Story

Here's another game to try. Circle a word in each line below. Then write the words in the numbered blanks of *The Deserted Hot Dog*. Try playing this game with a friend. Have fun reading your silly stories aloud!

1 goofy, harsh, happy

2 fed, dressed, wiggled

3 thank, bathe, tickle

4 cute, crazy, orange

5 stinky, miserable, hopeful

6 scared, walked, pet

7 grow, hear, know

8 muddy, silly, grumpy

9 lousy, friendly, rough

10 hug, smell, kiss

11 tough, fat, funny

Adopting a Dog

Congratulations on deciding to make a dog a part of your family! Remember to make adoption your first option! There are wonderful dogs in shelters across the country, waiting for a second chance to become a family member.

Here are some things to consider:

- Think long-term—your pet can be with you ten to fifteen years from now.

- Do you want a "go-getter," a "goofball," or a "couch potato"? Let the shelter staff help you make the best match for your family.

- Stock up on supplies before you bring your new pet home—shelter staff can guide you on what to get at the pet supply store or supermarket.

- Make sure you can set aside time each day for your dog. Create a family chart for doggy care duties.

- Dog-proof your home: for example, tuck electrical cords out of the way and make sure small toys and poisonous chemicals and plants are out of reach.

- The adult pets at the shelter can be a perfect choice — their sizes and personalities are fully developed, and most are already housebroken!

- Teach your dog good manners. The teaching process will bring you closer together, and a well-behaved pet will make you both happier!

You can visit **www.aspca.org/adopt** for more details on the adoption process and to find a shelter near you.

ASPCA
WE ARE THEIR VOICE®

Adoption tips provided courtesy of the American Society for the Prevention of Cruelty to Animals.

So You Want to Be a Dog?

Adaptation by Jamie White

Based on TV series teleplays

written by Raye Lankford and Peter K. Hirsch

Based on characters created by Susan Meddaugh

MARTHA SAYS HELLO

So you want to be a dog? Hey, who doesn't? But before you start hanging out at hydrants or barking at your friends, read this book to see what a dog's life is *really* like. You might be surprised to learn that it can be a little *ruff*. Take it from me, Martha!

Of course, I'm not exactly your common canine. Ever since Helen fed me her alphabet soup, I've been able to speak. And speak and speak . . . No one's sure how or why, but the letters in the soup traveled up to my brain instead of down to my stomach.

Now as long as I eat my daily bowl of alphabet soup, I can talk. To my family—Helen, baby Jake, Mom, Dad, and Skits, who only speaks Dog. To Helen's best human friend, T.D. To anyone who'll listen.

Sometimes my family wishes I didn't talk quite so much. But living with a talking dog has its perks. Like the time I entered a contest on the radio and won us a weekend at the Come-On-Inn!

And if I couldn't talk, I wouldn't be able to tell you this story. It's about what happened when two of my human friends became dogs for a day. Have *you* ever wanted to be a dog? Then you'd better read on . . .

Part One

DOG DAY AFTERNOON

If you're going to be a dog, then you'll want a good human. Helen is my human. We have lots of fun together. But when she hurt her ankle, all she could do was lie on the couch.

"Why don't you lick it?" I asked. "That's what I do when my paw hurts."

"I can't lick my ankle," said Helen.

"Want me to lick it?" I offered.

Helen scratched my head. "You're sweet, but—"

She was interrupted by the arrival of her cousin, Carolina. "Hey, lazybones!" Carolina teased. "What are you doing on the couch?"

"I sprained my ankle in gym class," Helen replied.

"Oh, I can totally empathize," said Carolina. "I once sprained my ankle running to the mall. My foot looked like an eggplant for a week, but I got the cutest shorts for half off."

"Mmm! What's in there?" I asked, sniffing the paper bag in her hand.

Carolina held it away from me. "Tamales. For *humans*."

Figures.

"My dad made them for our sleepover," she said, heading into the kitchen. She set her bag on the counter, where she saw a piece of paper. "Helen, did you see this note?"

"What's it say?" Helen called.

" 'Remember to take Martha to the vet,' "
read Carolina.

"Uh, that's trash," I said.

Helen sat up. "I completely forgot! Martha
has to go in for her shots."

"Don't be a hero, Helen!"
I pleaded. "Lie back down. The vet can wait till
you get better. Longer, even. Actually, forever!"

"Martha's right," said Carolina. "You shouldn't
put pressure on that ankle."

"Listen to Carolina," I said. "She knows what
she's talking about."

"I'll take Martha to the vet," Carolina offered.

"Don't listen to *her!*" I cried. "She doesn't know what she's talking about!"

But it was too late. "Come on, Martha," said Carolina. "I'll get the leash."

LEASH?! This day is getting worse by the minute, I thought. Dog Rule #15: At the first sight of a leash, RUN!

I bolted out the door.

"Martha, come here!" Carolina shouted, chasing me down the sidewalk. "I need you on the leash!"

I stopped. "Why?"

"So you don't run off."

"Me? Run off?"

But then I heard a *chitter-chatter* behind me. "SQUIRREL!" I shouted, running after it. Oh, yeah. There's nothing like chasing

a squirrel up a tree to make a dog forget her troubles.

"Martha, get over here!" Carolina ordered.

And I would have. Honest. If I hadn't smelled . . . "MEAT!" I cried, taking off again. I tracked the scent to a trash can, found a sandwich, and swallowed it in one gulp. "Mmm. Bologna!"

Carolina caught up with me. "Come here
NOW!"

"All right, all right. I will in— Whoa, MUD!"
I splashed into a gloopy puddle.

Ahhh! Mud, meat, and squirrels. What more
could a dog ask for? This day had really turned
around. Until a hand clipped the leash onto my
collar.

"Gotcha!" said Carolina.

I DON'T LIKE GOING TO THE VET

I don't like wearing a leash. I don't like going to the vet. I DON'T like wearing a leash to the vet. So why was Carolina the one moaning?

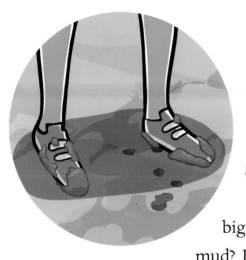

"Shoes! Mud!" she wailed, frowning at her feet. "MUD SHOES!"

What was the big woof about a little mud? I had just rolled my whole body in mud. It was delightful.

Carolina's mud shoes went *squelch, squelch* all the way to the vet's office. Even though it was my appointment, she lay on the doctor's table and winced.

The vet cleaned the mud off Carolina's shoes. "There," she said. "All done."

"Thanks, doc," I said, creeping toward the exit. "Send us a bill."

"Not yet," she said. "It's time for your shot."

She set me on the table and took out a long needle.

"I was afraid you'd say that," I said. "It's tough being a dog sometimes."

"I empathize," said the vet. "No, wait, I sympathize. I always get those two mixed up."

"Really?" I said. The needle loomed closer. "Wh-what's the difference?"

She paused. "Empathy means you know *exactly* what the other person feels because you've gone through the same thing yourself. For instance, I've had mud on my shoes, so I can empathize with what Carolina went through."

She leaned in again with my shot. Yikes! I had to distract her.

"Sympathy is something else?" I asked quickly.

The vet straightened. "Yes. It's sort of the same feeling, but slightly different. You feel sorry for what someone else is going through. But with sympathy, you haven't had the same thing happen to you."

"That is fascinating," I said, hopping off the table. "Well, thanks."

"Anytime, Martha," she replied.

I looked back at Carolina. "Let's go! I'll meet you outside. Hurry!" But when I turned to walk out the door, the vet was blocking it.

"Almost forgot one thing," she said, coming toward me, needle in hand.

The vet drew closer. I squeezed my eyes shut. I felt her hand on my neck. "Okay, doc, I'm ready for my shot."

"That's good, but I just gave it to you," she said.

"You did?" I opened my eyes.

"Hey, that wasn't so bad."

But for the record, I still do NOT like going to the vet.

IMPORTANT BUSINESS

On the way home, Carolina tugged at my leash.

"Come on," she said, frowning at the gray sky. "We have to get home. It's going to rain."

"I'm doing important business," I said.

"You're not doing anything. You're just sniffing."

"Don't pressure me," I said. "Empathize a little."

Carolina wrinkled her nose in disgust. "I don't know how you can sniff hydrants. Dogs have the most repellent mannerisms."

"I thought mannerisms were good," I said. "Like saying 'please' and 'thank you.'"

"That's manners," said Carolina. "Mannerisms are things you do a lot. Like if you wave your hands when you talk, or bite your fingernails when you're nervous."

I stopped at a fence. *Sniff!* "Ooo! Rinty was here," I said.

"Hurry up!" begged Carolina. "It's about to rain."

"I told you, I have important business."

"All you have is disgusting dog business," said Carolina. "Eating out of the trash, rolling in mud, sniffing everything."

"That's impor-
tant," I said.

"Not to me!"

"So?" I re-
plied.

Carolina
yanked my leash.
"So COME ON!"

I yanked back. "Maybe you should try to
have a little sympathy. Maybe you should try
walking on a leash! Maybe
you should see what
it's like to be a
dog!"

Suddenly, it
began to pour.

"Oh no!" cried Carolina. "I told you!"

We raced home. By the time we burst through the door, we were soaked. I shook myself off.

"Martha!" Carolina shrieked. "You're getting me even wetter!"

"Oops! Sorry," I said.

"I knew this was going to . . . to . . . ah-CHOOOO!" Carolina sneezed.

Mom came into the hall. "Oh my!" she said. "Let's get you into some dry clothes and a warm bed."

Carolina followed Mom upstairs.

"Hey, I'm wet and cold too," I called up after them. "Does anybody have sympathy for the dog? Anybody?"

Sigh.

That night, nobody could sleep. In her bed, Helen shifted her swollen ankle and moaned. Across from her, on an inflatable mattress, Carolina sneezed.

"Unggh," moaned Helen.

"Ah-choo!" sneezed Carolina.

"Unggh." "Ah-choo!" "Unggh." "Ah-choo!"

Some sleepover. It was going to be a long night.

THE UNEXPECTED GUEST

The next morning, I was awoken by an unfamiliar bark. I opened one eye and gasped. A collie was lying on Carolina's inflatable mattress!

Ruff-ruff! it barked. (Which in Dog means, "Wow, I feel so much better! Even though I had to sleep on the floor.")

"Um, hello?" I said. "Where did you come from?"

Helen sat up in bed. "Yeah, where *did* that dog come from?"

Ruff? The collie trotted over to the mirror and gaped at her reflection. "OH NO! I'M A DOG!" she howled. She ran in circles, barking like crazy.

That collie is cuckoo, I thought.

"Martha, you'd better get that collie out of here before Carolina sees it," said Helen. "You know she's not a fan of dogs."

Ruff, ruff! barked the collie.

"She says she *is* Carolina." I laughed. "As if."

Ruff! Ruff!

"She says she just woke up as a dog," I told Helen.

I gave the collie a sniff. She didn't smell human. But there was one way to know for

sure. "Let me ask you a question," I said. "Dogs should be on leashes. True or False?"

Ruff!

I gasped. *"True?!* You *are* Carolina!"

For a second opinion, we called Truman, who'd memorized the characteristics of 203 dog breeds, and invited him over. He brought his doctor's kit and T.D., who just had to see Collie Carolina for himself.

"Say aaaah!" said Truman, holding a tongue depressor in front of her.

She opened her mouth. Truman cringed. "Ack! You have bad breath," he said. "But that's characteristic of dogs."

"Characteristic?" I said.

"Characteristics are the things that are special about how you look or act," said Truman. "Carolina has all the characteristics of a dog. She's furry, has four paws and a tail, and barks."

Ruff!

"Carolina says she doesn't want to have the characteristics of a dog," I said. "She wants us to switch her back into a human."

RUFF! RUFF!

"As soon as possible," I added.

Helen hugged her cousin. "Don't worry. We'll get you back to your old self."

"If we can figure out how Carolina became a dog," said Truman, "maybe we can reverse it."

"I've got it!" said T.D. "Maybe she was bitten by some weird half-dog, half-kid creature under a full moon?"

"You're not saying . . ." said Truman.

"Carolina's a WEREDOG!" T.D. exclaimed.

"Hmm. What are the characteristics of a weredog?" asked Truman.

T.D. shrugged. "Like werewolves, I guess. Only doggier."

"Good theory," said Truman, "but there wasn't a full moon last night."

Only Truman would know that, I thought.

T.D. tried again. "Maybe Carolina switched places with a dog. Right now, somewhere out there, there's a dog living in Carolina's body."

"So somewhere the human Carolina is chasing sticks and rolling in mud?" I asked.

Collie Carolina shuddered.

"I'm sure a dog didn't switch places with you," Helen reassured her. "At least, I hope not."

While we were thinking, Carolina began scratching herself.

Truman shone a light into her ears. "It's just what I thought," he said grimly. "I'm afraid there's no easy way to say this."

"What?" asked Helen, alarmed.

"Carolina," Truman announced, "has fleas."

DOG DAZE

"I can empathize," I told Carolina. "Even the best of us get fleas sometimes. But, uh, I'll just stand way over here, okay?" I took a big step back.

Suddenly, Carolina sniffed the air. *Ruff?*

"Mmm. I smell it too," I said. "Come on!"

We ran out the doggie door, following a delicious scent. It led us to the garbage.

"Ooh, look! A burger!" I said. "Dig in!"

Carolina wrinkled her nose. *Ruff!*

"Gross?" I repeated. "You're a dog now. You should learn to cherish these moments when it's just you and the trash."

But Carolina wasn't listening. She was staring at a squirrel. Her legs twitched. But she didn't move.

"Carolina, chasing squirrels is what dogs do," I said. "They're just mannerisms, right? We can't help ourselves. You're a dog now. Trust your instincts."

Trusting *my* instincts, I began eating from the trash.

Too soon, Helen showed up. "Martha!" she cried. "You know you're not supposed to go through the trash."

Next to me, Carolina froze.

"*Carolina?* Bad girl!" Helen scolded. Then she blushed. "I can't believe I'm talking to my cousin like this."

Ruff! Ruff!

"What did she say?" Helen asked.

"She said she's starting to see things from a dog's point of view," I said. "Does that mean she's seeing things from down here?"

Helen shook her head. "A point of view is the way you understand things. When Carolina says she can see things from your point of view, she means she understands them the way you do."

This was true. Because when another squirrel darted by, Carolina didn't hesitate to chase it.

"Carolina!" shouted Helen.

"Heel, girl!" ordered Truman.

"Come back!" called T.D.

We all ran after her. But Carolina was faster. She chased the squirrel . . . then a rabbit . . . and then a car. Her *dad's* car.

"Hey, that's my papi," she barked, running after him. "Dad!"

Carolina followed the car all the way to her father's market. When he stepped out, she jumped up to greet him.

Ruff, ruff, ruff, ruff, ruff!

"Ai-yi-yi!" said her dad, pushing her away. "Shoo! Go away, dog!"

"Papi, it's me, Carolina!" she yipped. But he didn't understand Dog.

He hurried into his store. Carolina whimpered outside. She was so upset, she didn't notice Kazuo drive up.

DOGGY EVER AFTER

We were still searching for Carolina when we met her father sweeping in front of his market. We told him that his daughter was now a dog.

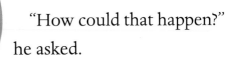

"How could that happen?" he asked.

"She was either bitten by a weredog," I said, "or she's just really lucky."

"I don't care if Carolina is a dog," he said. "She's my daughter and I love her. We must find her!"

We all split up to search again. This time, I went to my doggie pals, who were on their way to the hydrant.

"We're looking for Carolina. She's a collie," I told them. "No tags, and— Wait a minute! NO TAGS! I know where she is!"

I raced to the animal shelter. Sure enough, a sad-eyed Carolina lay in a cage beside the front desk. I explained to Kazuo why he had to let her go.

"So you see," I said, "that collie isn't a real dog. She's a person."

"I totally sympathize," said Kazuo. "But if I let every dog that thought it was human out of the shelter, this place would be empty."

"What if I adopt her?" I suggested.

Kazuo shook his head. "That's against section six, rule nineteen of the Dog Shelter

Code: A dog cannot adopt another dog. Even if that dog can speak."

"You just made up that part about speaking, didn't you?" I asked.

"Well, uh . . ."

Before he could answer, Carolina's dad and the kids arrived. "There she is!" he said, rushing to her side. "This dog is my daughter! Release her immediately!"

Kazuo looked at Carolina, and then back at her dad. "Well, she does have your eyes," he admitted.

So we finally got to take her home.

Now Carolina enjoys life as a dog. She plays fetch with her dad, chases squirrels, and splashes in mud puddles. And since dogs don't wear clothes, she doesn't even miss the mall.

Best of all, her dad loves her no matter what. "Even though you're a dog," he says, "I still cherish you."

And they lived happily ever after.

REWIND

Gah. Truman wants me to tell the rest of the story. What's wrong with Carolina being a dog forever? I think that's a dream come true, don't you? But it *was* only a dream. Okay, here's what really happened.

The morning after the sleepover, I woke up to find Carolina crawling to the mirror. She stopped to scratch behind her ear with her toes.

"Uh, hello?" I said.

She looked up. Then she noticed her reflection and smiled. "I'm me!" she exclaimed. "It must have been a dream. What a relief!"

What's a relief? I wondered. *And why is she acting so . . . doggish?*

"Want to go for a walk?" she asked me. "Huh? Huh? Huh?"

"Uh, sure," I answered. "But I don't do leashes."

"Me neither," said Carolina. "No way! I totally understand your point of view."

"Are you *sure* you feel okay?" I asked.

"Yes. And I can empathize with you now."

Helen sat up and stretched. "Who wants breakfast?" she asked.

Skits and I rushed to her side. *Woof, woof, woof!* we barked.

"*Woof*—I mean, me, me, me!" said Carolina, joining us dogs.

I was a little worried that this new Carolina might eat breakfast out of my dog bowl, but she was back to her old self soon enough. *Except* when she sees a squirrel. (Leaping lasagna, can that girl run!)

Part Two

THE DEAL

Make no bones about it, I love being a dog. But as you can see, it's not always a walk in the park. Take what happened to T.D., for example. It all started when Helen and I found him sulking on his front step.

"What's the matter?" she asked.

T.D. sighed. "It's Saturday."

"Isn't that a good thing?" Helen asked.

"No," said T.D. "Saturday leads to Sunday, which leads to Monday, and you know what that means."

"Free pineapple topping at Mario's Pizza?" said Helen.

"Nope. School," said T.D. "Let me give you some highlights from this week. Or in my case, *low*lights."

His troubles began on Monday morning when his homework flew out the bus window.

On Tuesday, he'd set his lunch on a bench, where Alvin Merkel accidentally sat on it.

On Wednesday, he got locked in the utility closet. The janitor had to let him out, which Tiffany Blatsky thought was hilarious.

"On Thursday," said T.D., "Alvin Merkel—"

"Sat on your lunch again?" said Helen.

"No," said T.D. "He ran into Billy Taber, who sat on my lunch."

"And yesterday?" said Helen.

"The worst day of all!" cried T.D. He told us that during Mrs. Clusky's science class, he'd been drawing instead of paying attention.

"Based on the results of our experiment," she told the class, "we draw a conclusion. The conclusion is what we've found out. What's our conclusion about what happens when you mix baking soda and vinegar? T.D.?"

He looked up from his sketchbook. "Um, toothpaste?"

Mrs. Clusky frowned. "Perhaps you'll be less distracted when you present your own science project on Monday."

T.D. groaned at the memory. "Ugh, school! I wish I never had to go."

I tried to sympathize, but something caught my eye. "SQUIRREL!" I whooped, taking off after it.

"Why couldn't I have been born a dog?" sighed T.D. "Dogs have it easy."

I stopped short. "Did I just hear you say 'Dogs have it *easy*'?"

"No school? No science projects? Compared to people, dogs have it super easy," said T.D.

"Try being me for a day and see how easy it is," I dared him.

"Try being *me* for a day and see how easy it

is," said T.D.

"Deal!"

"Deal!"

We stared each other down, nose to wet nose.

"Wait, what just happened?" asked T.D.

Helen giggled. "You agreed to be Martha for a day and she agreed to be you."

"Great!" said T.D. "I feel better already. Tomorrow, I'm a dog all day long."

"And Monday, I'll be the newest student at Wag-staff City Elementary School," I said.

DOG FOR A DAY

T.D. went home to tell his dad, O.G., about our deal. He'd found him in the garage, working on one of his latest inventions.

"Hmm," said O.G. "So you think it's easier being a dog than a person? I'd say you have an unusual hypothesis."

T.D. looked frightened. "*I do?* Is it contagious?"

O.G. laughed. "No. A hypothesis is a guess or idea about what you think might happen. But to find out if you're right or not, you must conduct an experiment."

"An experiment? Like with microscopes and test tubes?"

"That's one kind of experiment," said O.G. "But an experiment can be any way of testing an idea."

"Or hypothesis," said T.D.

"Exactly! When I was your age, I had

a hypothesis that I could fuel a go-cart on root beer."

"Did it work?" T.D. asked.

"It might have, if I hadn't gotten thirsty," O.G. replied. "The question is, what do you need to change about yourself to become a dog? Let's compare."

"Okay," said T.D., pulling out his sketchbook.

"Dogs are warm-blooded," said O.G.

"I'm warm-blooded," said T.D., drawing himself and a dog.

"They have fur or hair."

"Check," said T.D.

"They chew on bones," added O.G.

"I enjoy a bone."

"Zounds!" said O.G., looking at T.D.'s sketch. "Maybe you're already a dog. Except . . ."

"Except?" said T.D.

"Dogs don't draw."

T.D. gulped. "No problem," he said, gently placing the sketchbook on the workbench. "I can go a day without drawing. This is going to be easy."

O.G.'s eyes lit up. "Wait! I have it!"

"Have what?" asked T.D.

"A tail."

T.D.'s jaw dropped. "*You* have a tail?"

"No, *you*," said O.G. "To be a dog, you'll need a tail. I'll invent one for you. Don't go anywhere!"

"I'll just be over here, scratching behind my ears with my paw," said T.D. "Ow!"

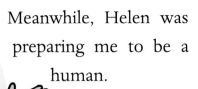

Meanwhile, Helen was preparing me to be a human.

"So let's review what people do and compare that with dogs," she said. "A lot of humans work or, like T.D., they go to school."

I looked up from my bowl. "I was a substitute teacher once."

"Humans eat three meals a day," Helen continued.

"I am eager to try this bonus meal they call lunch," I said.

Just then, a squirrel hopped onto the windowsill. "Uh, excuse me. I have to get this."

WOOF! WOOF! I barked at it.

"*And,*" Helen shouted, "humans don't chase squirrels."

"Right," I said. "Okay. I can go a day without chasing squirrels. Being a human for a day is going to be easy."

NO T.D.s ALLOWED

The next morning, T.D.'s dad was waiting for him in the kitchen.

"Good morning!" said O.G. "Or should I say 'woof-woof'?"

T.D. looked confused.

"Your experiment?" O.G. reminded him. "Dog for a day?"

"Oh, right! I almost forgot," said T.D., dropping to his hands and knees.

"I didn't," I said. T.D. did a double-take. "Just here to observe."

"I'm putting the final touches on your tail," said O.G. He held up a mechanical tail and remote control. "Observe. That means 'watch very closely.'"

He pressed a button and—*whirrrr!* The tail whipped wildly and flew out of his hands.

"Agh!" cried T.D., ducking. The tail skimmed his head and whizzed out of the room.

"Uh, small adjustment necessary," O.G. said. "Anyway, it's time for your breakfast." He set a dog bowl on the floor.

"What's this?" T.D. asked.

"Alphabet soup. Just like Martha eats. It's either that or dog food."

T.D. studied the bowl. "I guess dogs don't use spoons."

"Nope," I said. "Just lean in and lap away."

"Great! Less to clean up," said T.D. He dove in with a loud *slurp!* I have to admit, I was impressed.

"All done!" he said, not bothering to wipe his face. "Now, what should I do today? Oh, that's right. I'm a dog, which means I can do . . . whatever I want!"

T.D. was a natural. He played fetch. He rolled in the grass. He even chewed a rubber bone—and *liked* it.

"I love being a dog!" he said. "What else do dogs do all day?"

"Root through the trash behind the grocery store?" I suggested.

"Maybe later. What else?" T.D. asked.

"Run after passing cars?"

"Sounds dangerous," he said. "I know! I'll go see if some of my friends can play. That's something dogs do."

First we went to my house. But Helen was busy cleaning her room. Then we visited Truman. But he was helping his dad take newspapers to the recycling center.

"New hypothesis," said T.D. as we headed home. "Humans devote too much time to chores."

"Ready to give up?" I asked.

"No way," said T.D. "It proves my point. People have it harder than dogs."

The darkening sky rumbled. "Uh-oh. Looks like rain," I said.

"No problem," said T.D. "I'll hang out at the library."

"Don't think so," I said. "Dogs don't have library cards. And . . . well, you'll see."

At the library, T.D. stared at the sign on the front door.

"No dogs allowed?" he said. "That doesn't seem fair."

"Now that you're a dog, T.D., you're going to discover the one thing every canine knows: it's a human world we live in."

With that, it began to pour.

"Human or canine," said T.D., "we have to get out of the rain. And we're pretty far from home."

"Looks like I'll have to teach a new dog old tricks," I said. We waited out the storm underneath the porch of a nearby house. After a while, T.D.'s stomach growled.

"Hope it stops soon," said T.D. "It's almost lunchtime."

"Hate to be the one to break it to you, but dogs don't eat lunch. Unless you happen to sniff out something yummy in a trash can," I said.

"Ew," said T.D.

"Ready to admit that it's harder being a dog?" I asked.

T.D. chased his imaginary tail before settling down again. "Just wait till you have to be a human tomorrow and go to school," he said. "I think you'll come to a very different conclusion."

DOGS DON'T DRAW

Back at T.D.'s house, we shook off the rain.

"Now I'm really hungry," he said, reaching for the refrigerator.

"Not so fast," I warned. "You do know dogs can't open refrigerator doors, right?"

"Uh, right," said T.D. "No problem."

"If you bark, someone may eventually get annoyed enough to feed you."

"HUNGRY!" he hollered at once. "VERY HUNGRY!"

O.G. appeared in the doorway with a new mechanical tail. "T.D.! Just the dog I was

looking for," he said. "It's time for your dinner."

O.G. placed a bowl on the floor.

"Soup again?" moaned T.D.

"Dogs don't have much variety in their meals," I explained.

"Soup it is," said T.D. He planted his face in the bowl.

About this time, Helen arrived. She giggled at the sight of T.D. "How's the great dog-for-a-day experiment going?" she asked.

"Kind of messy," said T.D. "But it's a lot easier than being in school."

O.G. attached the mechanical tail to the back of T.D.'s pants. "Finished!" he said. "Observe."

He clicked the remote control. The tail began to twirl, faster and faster. Suddenly, it lifted into the air, nearly taking T.D.'s pants with it. *Snap!* went his waistband.

"Owwww!" howled T.D.

The tail flew out the kitchen window. We watched O.G. chase it around the yard.

"Now that's something you don't see every day," I said. "A human chasing his tail."

Helen decided that was her cue to go. After
she left, T.D. reached for his sketchbook on the
coffee table.

"Uh-uh," I said.

"What?" he asked.

"I thought maybe you were about to draw."

"No way!" T.D. protested. "Everyone knows
dogs don't draw. I'll just be over here scratching
behind my ears."

He plopped down, repeating to himself, "Dogs don't draw. Dogs don't draw. Dogs don't draw."

That night, curled up in a dog bed, he was still murmuring it in his sleep.

SO YOU STILL WANT TO BE A DOG?

The next morning, Helen found T.D. sketching in the schoolyard.

"You really missed drawing, didn't you?" she asked.

"A little bit," he said. "Where's Martha?"

Helen shrugged. "She wasn't at breakfast."

"Aha!" said T.D., smiling. "She's only been a human for an hour and she's already late. Not like being a dog, where you don't have to be anywhere on time."

But when they walked into homeroom, they were in for a surprise.

"Hi, guys!" I said.

"Martha! You're here," said Helen.

Yup. Not only was I at school, but it turns out I'm pretty good at it. I didn't even eat my homework. Helen was proud. T.D. wasn't as pleased.

After class, he grumbled, "Martha knew the capital of South Dakota. How did she do that?"

"Martha's smart," said Helen.

"Maybe my hypothesis was wrong," said T.D. "It's a lot easier for Martha to be a human than it was for me to be a dog."

"Don't jump to any conclusions," said Helen. "The experiment isn't over yet."

"Maybe not. But I can already see the results," he said.

T.D. joined me outside for lunch. I was enjoying the contents of my own paper bag.

"Mmm!" I said, licking my chops. "People have come up with some great inventions. But the best one ever is lunch."

T.D. took a bite out of his sandwich and sighed. "The results are not good," he said.

"That's okay. I'll eat them," I offered.

"Results aren't food," said T.D. "A result is what happens when you do something."

"Oh, like as a result of eating lunch, I'm happy?" I asked.

"Yes. And the results of this experiment show that you were right about being a dog," he said. "It is easier to be a person than to be a dog. I was a very bad dog." He scolded himself: "Bad dog!"

"You're not a bad dog," I said, jumping up beside him. "Can I tell you a secret? Being a human hasn't been easy at all."

"It hasn't?" asked T.D.

"No, it was hard," I confessed. "I had to memorize all those state capitals, get up early, and you're not even allowed to fall asleep in class."

"Tell me about it," said T.D.

"I'd say your experiment has taught us a lot."

"Experiment!" he cried. "Oh no! I'm supposed to present a science project this afternoon!"

"Didn't we just *live* a pretty good science experiment?" I asked.

"You're right!" T.D. exclaimed. He grabbed his sketchbook and wrote:

Hypothesis: It's easier being a dog than a person.

Later that day, he presented his science project to the class.

"So the conclusion of my experiment is that it's just as hard to be dog as it is to be a person. But either way," T.D. said, smiling at Helen and me, "it's easier if you have friends."

Woof! I barked in agreement. Having human *and* canine friends made me one lucky dog!

From then on, T.D. and Carolina never thought dogs had it easy again. But hey, you don't have to take their word for it. You can try being a dog for a day too. Maybe even . . . today!

(Just remember, no eating your homework!)

GLOSSARY

How many words do you remember from the story?

characteristic: something that is special about how you look or act

conclusion: what you've found out from an experiment

empathy: knowing what another person feels because you've gone through the same thing yourself

experiment: any way of testing an idea

hypothesis: a guess or idea about what you think might happen

mannerism: a gesture or action you do a lot

observe: to watch very closely

point of view: the way you understand things

result: what happens when you do something

sympathy: feeling sorry for what someone else is going through even though you haven't had the same thing happen to you

MARTHA'S DOG-FOR-A-DAY
EXPERIMENT

Ever wonder what life is like from a pooch's point of view? Then conduct your own dog-for-a-day experiment!

Here's what to do:

Step 1

Observe the behavior of humans and dogs. Compare their characteristics and mannerisms in a notebook, just like T.D. did.

Step 2

Next, write down your hypothesis. If you need help, simply fill in the blank: Dogs are more _____ than humans.

Step 3

Pick a day to be a dog. (Martha suggests a weekend. Dogs don't go to school!) Tell your family and friends so they can play along.

Step 4

On the day of your experiment, act like a dog from morning to bedtime.

Step 5

When you're done, record the results and your conclusion. Were they what you expected? What kind of dog were you? Draw a picture!

PICK-ME-UP
POOCH

If you feel sympathy or empathy for someone, show them you care with a dog card.

1 Fold a square piece of paper in half to make a triangle.

2 Fold two corners of the triangle down to make ears.

3 Draw some eyes, a nose, and a mouth. Write your message on the back or under one of the ears!